BIGGER DIGGER

STEVE WEBB ★ BEN MANTLE

PICTURE CORGI

Big lorry, quarry lorry,

splish, splash, **muck.**

Quarry lorry,

big lorry,

Slip, slide, **stuck!**

Dump truck,
tow truck,

pull us from the **yucky muck.**

Heave-ho, dump truck,
quarry lorry **push.**

Splish, splash, mud bath,
mud bath **mush!**

Oh no! Dump truck, quarry lorry push,

Quarry lorry, dump truck,

slip, slide, muck.

dump truck, tow truck,
sinking in the **mush.**

Dump truck, quarry lorry,
sink,
sunk, stuck!

Little yellow dumper digger!

Everybody shout!

Dumper digger, yellow digger,
please dig us out!

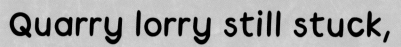

Quarry lorry still stuck,

dump truck too,

dig, little yellow digger,
little digger do!

Dig down, dig **around**,
digging in the
muddy ground.

Heave-ho!
CRASH
BASH!

Dig a bigger
splish splash,

Oh no! Slip, slide, mud bath **mash,**

little yellow dumper digger upside down ...

Quarry lorry,   dump truck,

little digger too,

all **stuck,**
still stuck,
whatever will
they **do?**

Bigger digger,

dumper digger,
to the rescue!

Dig, bigger dumper digger,

bigger digger, **do!**

Down, down,
deep down,
dig down deep.
Dig a bigger
deep down,
big mud
heap.

Roll over, little digger,
bigger digger push.
Little digger unstuck,
out of the mush!

Dig, bigger dumper digger,
little digger, do!

Dump truck, quarry lorry,
unstuck too!

Thank you, bigger dumper digger!
Everybody shout! Let's do it all again,
and dig each other **out!**

For Charlie and Harry, with love and mud
– Steve Webb

For David, Arthur and Theodore
and for little digger Louis
– Ben Mantle

BIGGER DIGGER
A PICTURE CORGI BOOK 978 0 552 57588 1
Published in Great Britain by Picture Corgi, an imprint of Random House Children's Books
A Random House Group Company
This edition published 2012
1 3 5 7 9 10 8 6 4 2
Text copyright © Steve Webb, 2012
Illustrations copyright © Ben Mantle, 2012
The right of Steve Webb and Ben Mantle to be identified as the author and illustrator of
this work has been asserted in accordance with the Copyright, Designs and Patents Act 1988.
All rights reserved. No part of this publication may be reproduced, stored in a retrieval system,
or transmitted in any form or by any means, electronic, mechanical, photocopying,
recording or otherwise, without the prior permission of the publishers.
RANDOM HOUSE CHILDREN'S BOOKS, 61–63 Uxbridge Road, London W5 5SA
www.kidsatrandomhouse.co.uk
www.randomhouse.co.uk
Addresses for companies within The Random House Group Limited can be found at:
www.randomhouse.co.uk/offices.htm
THE RANDOM HOUSE GROUP Limited Reg. No. 954009
A CIP catalogue record for this book is available from the British Library.
Printed in China